Adapted by Mary Tillworth
Based on the original screenplay by Steve Granat & Cydne Clark
Illustrated by Ulkutay Design Group

Special thanks to Sarah Buzby, Cindy Ledermann, Ann McNeill, Dana Koplik, Emily Kelly, Sharon Woloszyk, Tanya Mann, Julia Phelps, Rita Lichtwardt, Kathy Berry, Rob Hudnut, David Wiebe, Shelley Dvi-Vardhana, Michelle Cogan, Gabrielle Miles, Rainmaker Entertainment, and Walter P. Martishius

 A GOLDEN BOOK • NEW YORK

BARBIE and associated trademarks and trade dress are owned by, and used under license from, Mattel, Inc.
Copyright © 2012 Mattel, Inc. All Rights Reserved.
www.barbie.com
Published in the United States by Golden Books, an imprint of Random House Children's Books, a division of Random House, Inc., 1745 Broadway, New York, NY 10019, and in Canada by Random House of Canada Limited, Toronto. No part of this book may be reproduced or copied in any form without permission from the copyright owner. Golden Books, A Golden Book, A Little Golden Book, the G colophon, and the distinctive gold spine are registered trademarks of Random House, Inc.
randomhouse.com/kids
Educators and librarians, for a variety of teaching tools, visit us at randomhouse.com/teachers
ISBN: 978-0-307-97617-8
Printed in the United States of America
10 9 8 7

In the magical land of Meribella, a lovely princess named Tori was greeting a long line of royal visitors. They had come for a festival to celebrate the kingdom's five hundredth anniversary. As she curtseyed yet again, Tori wished she could escape her princess duties and have more fun. What she really wanted was the exciting life of a pop star.

Not far away, a pop star named Keira was singing to a crowd of adoring fans. Keira loved performing day after day, but she wished she had more time to write new songs. She wanted to live the carefree life of a princess.

The next day, members of the royal court were invited to the palace to meet the royal family. Keira was on the guest list and was going to perform at the festival. The pop star and Tori instantly became friends. Even their dogs, Riff and Vanessa, got along well.

Tori gave Keira a tour of the palace, and soon the girls were joking about trading places. Keira showed Tori the magic microphone her aunt had given her. She used it to transform her dress into a royal gown.

"I have something like that," Tori said. She pulled out her magic hairbrush and gave herself a rockin' hairstyle.

Keira and Tori stared at each other. "You look just like me!" they said at the same time.

Disguised as each other, the pop star and the princess continued to explore the palace. They entered a secret garden where fairies were tending a beautiful plant covered with flowering diamonds.

"This is the magical Diamond Gardenia," Tori told Keira. "Its roots spread throughout the kingdom. Without it, Meribella would wither and die."

While Keira and Tori admired the Gardenia, they found two diamonds that had dropped to the ground. The fairies used the diamonds to make a star necklace for Keira and a heart necklace for Tori.

Just then, Tori got an idea. She asked Keira to trade places with her for a day. "It'd be magical! I'd get to be a pop star, and you'd get to be a princess!"

The two girls were so excited, they didn't notice Keira's greedy manager, Crider, peering into the garden.

The next morning, Tori got her chance to live the life of Keira the pop star! During dance practice, she twirled and spun to the music—and loved every minute of it.

Meanwhile, Keira was having the time of her life pretending to be Princess Tori. As she rode through the kingdom in the royal carriage, Keira felt freer than ever before.

The princess and the pop star were having so much fun being each other, they decided to do it for one more day!

The next day, Tori—disguised as Keira—walked through the streets of Meribella for the first time. Girls rushed to get her autograph. They told Tori that their families didn't have the money to buy tickets to the festival. Tori decided to arrange for all the children of Meribella to see the concert for free.

At the palace, Keira was having a blast pretending to be Princess Tori. But she wasn't very princesslike when she put her feet up on the breakfast table! Keira was locked in her bedroom as punishment.

The night of the festival, both girls were in trouble. Keira was still locked in the princess's bedroom—and Tori wasn't ready to perform at the concert! Keira tried to call Tori—just as Tori tried to call her! The girls missed each other's calls.

 Knowing that the concert meant a lot to Keira, Tori went onstage. She was nervous, but she took a deep breath and sang a sweet, beautiful song to a hushed audience. When she was finished, there was a moment of silence . . . and then the crowd went wild!

Meanwhile, Crider and his assistant, Rupert, had snuck into the palace's secret garden. Rupert pulled the Diamond Gardenia plant out of the ground while Crider gathered every last diamond. "Now let's make our escape!" Crider crowed.

With the Diamond Gardenia uprooted, all plant life around Meribella had begun to wither and die. Tori gasped as the flowers turned brown and wilted in her hands. "Something's wrong. . . . The Diamond Gardenia!" she cried. Tori dashed offstage and changed back into a princess.

Meanwhile, Keira had escaped from Tori's room and changed back into her regular self. She joined Tori just as Crider and Rupert were escaping in the royal carriage.

Tori stopped the carriage and Keira grabbed the Diamond Gardenia.

Tori and Keira rushed the Gardenia to the secret garden and tried to replant it, but it was too late. Soon all magic would disappear from Meribella—forever.

"Can't you plant another Gardenia?" asked Keira.

Tori shook her head. "Its diamonds were its seeds. If there were any diamonds left, we could plant them."

Suddenly, the two girls realized there *were*
two diamonds left—the ones on their necklaces!
They quickly planted the diamonds, and two new
Gardenias sprang up. All the magical life returned
to Meribella, and the kingdom was saved!

The princess and the pop star returned to the stage together to finish the concert. But before Keira started singing, she turned to Tori. "I think this song would be better as a duet," she said, and the two friends sang in perfect harmony.

Switching places had been fun, but Keira and Tori knew they needed to get back to their own lives. The princess and the pop star joined hands and promised to be friends forever.